ALFIE

Alfie and the Big Boys

For all children who will soon be starting school

Other titles in the Alfie series:

Alfie Gets in First

Alfie's Feet

Alfie Gives a Hand

An Evening at Alfie's

Alfie and the Birthday Surprise

Alfie Wins a Prize

Alfie Weather

Alfie's World

Annie Rose is my Little Sister

Rhymes for Annie Rose

The Big Alfie and Annie Rose Storybook

The Big Alfie Out of Doors Storybook

ALFIE AND THE BIG BOYS
A RED FOX BOOK 978 0 099 48844 6

First published in Great Britain by The Bodley Head, an imprint of Random House Children's Books
A Random House Group Company

The Bodley Head edition published 2007
This Red Fox edition published 2009

1 3 5 7 9 10 8 6 4 2

Copyright © Shirley Hughes, 2007

The right of Shirley Hughes to be identified as the author and illustrator of this work has been asserted in accordance
with the Copyright, Designs and Patents Act 1988.

Red Fox Books are published by Random House Children's Books, 61–63 Uxbridge Road, London W5 5SA

www.kidsatrandomhouse.co.uk
www.rbooks.co.uk

Addresses for companies within The Random House Group Limited can be found at: www.randomhouse.co.uk/offices.htm

THE RANDOM HOUSE GROUP Limited Reg. No. 954009

A CIP catalogue record for this book is available from the British Library.

Printed in Singapore

ALFIE

Alfie and the Big Boys

Shirley Hughes

Red Fox

In the mornings Alfie went to Nursery School. His friends Bernard, Min, Sara and Sam and the others went there too.

There were some
interesting things
to do at Nursery
School.

Alfie drew pictures and
learned how to write his
name at the top.

He did counting
and played
in the shop.

He sat on the floor with all the other children and listened to stories.

They sang songs together.

And sometimes they made
masks or paper crowns
to take home.

Alfie's Nursery School was right next door to the Big School, where Alfie and the others would go when they were older.

From their play area they could see the big children when they came out to play. Alfie and Bernard knew the names of some of the boys at Big School. There was Kevin Turley and Mohammed Rehan, Todd Rawlings and the Santos twins – who lived in Alfie's street. There was also a big boy with red hair whose name was Ian Barger.

Bernard liked Ian a lot, and laughed and laughed at the funny things he did. But Ian never took any notice of the little kids.

All the boys in Year One wanted to be in Ian's gang. Mostly they played football. Sometimes they pulled their sweaters over their heads and tore through the playground, hanging onto each other and pretending to be a fierce dragon.

They kept falling over on purpose and sometimes pulled other people over with them. Ian was always the one in front.

Bernard and Alfie both wished they could join in and be part of the fierce dragon too.

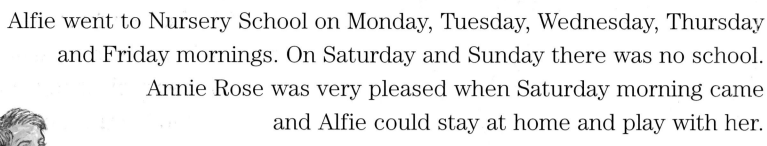

Alfie went to Nursery School on Monday, Tuesday, Wednesday, Thursday and Friday mornings. On Saturday and Sunday there was no school. Annie Rose was very pleased when Saturday morning came and Alfie could stay at home and play with her.

One fine Saturday morning Mum said she was going to take Alfie and Annie Rose with her to a pot plant sale. It was at a big house, not too far away. Alfie and Annie Rose had just started a good game and they didn't think pot plants sounded very interesting. But Dad was too busy to look after them that morning, so off they went.

The house where the pot plant sale was had a beautiful garden with shady paths and big trees and lots of flowers.

But Alfie and Annie Rose soon got bored
with watching Mum choose pot plants.

Luckily, there was a grassy place at the end of the garden, where helpers were looking after some children who were playing on swings and a climbing frame and a slide. Mum asked Alfie if he would like to stay there for a little while and he said yes.

So Mum went off with Annie Rose, saying that they would be back very soon.

Alfie had not been there very long when a great commotion broke out. Somebody was screaming and yelling and making a terrible fuss.

All the helpers were crowded around.

Right in the middle of them was a boy with a runny nose and
tears pouring down his cheeks, yelling at the top of his voice.
"I want my mummy! I want my mummy!" he shouted.

The kind helpers were trying to comfort him but he just went on yelling, "I want my MUMMY!"

"Don't worry, we'll soon find her for you," said one.

"Tell us your name, dear, will you?" said another.

But the boy would not tell them his name. He was far too busy yelling and sobbing.

"Doesn't anyone know his name?" cried one helper.

Only one person knew who that boy was. And that person was Alfie.

"I know who he is," he told everybody. "His name is Ian Barger and he goes to Parkside School."

As soon as Ian caught sight of Alfie, he grabbed him and held onto him very tightly. Then, slowly, he stopped crying and began sniffing and hiccupping instead.

Just at that moment, who should come hurrying up, red in the face, but Ian's mum.

"Oh dear, oh dear, what a fuss!" she said. "I told you I would be just over there buying a pot of geraniums!" Then she gave Ian a big hug and wiped his nose. "Poor little Ian!" she said. "Did you think you had lost me when I was right over there all the time?" Ian nodded his head. He was still hiccupping and holding tightly onto Alfie's hand.

"Well, I see you had a kind friend to look after you so you needn't have been frightened, need you, sweetheart?" said Ian's mum. And she beamed at Alfie.

Then she thanked the helpers and thanked Alfie specially for taking care of Ian. "How lucky you were here!" she told him.

Afterwards, she and Alfie's mum
had a chat. When it was time to
go, she bought all three
children ice creams. Ian was
now holding onto her hand
very firmly indeed.

At school next Monday morning Ian came swaggering out to play with the other boys, as usual. And, as usual, he took no notice of Alfie and Bernard. But when the ball bounced over into their bit of the playground and Alfie threw it back, he said, "Thanks, mate!"

Alfie's mum became friendly with Ian's mum while they waited together outside the school gates. One day Mum invited her to bring Ian for tea after school. Bernard was invited too.

"Better lock up all the breakables!" said Dad when he heard that Bernard *and* Ian were coming to tea.

But after tea they all went outside and had a great game together being big, tough boys!

But, as it turned out, Ian
did not break anything at all.
He spent most of his time
playing with Annie Rose.
He helped her to line up
her dolls and cuddly toys
into a football team and she
told him all their names.
Then they made a house
for them out of cushions.

Bernard and Alfie thought
that was a very babyish game.

"We love that story, don't we Moonlight?"
    Charlotte said.
"And I know why," said Mummy.
"We love it because it is about us,"
    Charlotte said. "Moonlight
        and Mummy and me."

"You've forgotten the best bit,"
said Charlotte. "Her mummy said
if no one owned the kitten they
could keep him for ever. She said
they should find a good name for
the kitten and the little girl knew
straightaway what it should be.
'Moonlight would be a good name,'
she told her mummy. 'We'd never
have found him without the
moonlight.'"

"So that's what they called their
kitten," Mummy said. "Now you've
told me the end of your story."

"She gave the kitten some warm milk and he went to sleep in her arms. And after a while the little girl felt sleepy too, and her mummy carried her and the kitten upstairs. She tucked the little girl in her bed all cosy and—"

"...and the little girl carried him all the way home."

"A little white kitten," said
Mummy, "all thin and bony
and cold. It was on a stone
with the sea splashing round
it. The poor little kitten was
hungry and scared. The little
girl and her mummy got
splashed. But they rescued
the kitten..."

"The little girl and her mummy walked out on the rocks. There was only the moonlight to see by. They walked right out by the edge of the sea – and what do you think they saw there?"

"It was a kitten!" said Charlotte.

"The little girl and her mummy went down to the shore." Charlotte said.

"Yes," Mummy said. "They searched and they searched but they couldn't find anything. 'Something *was* here,' said the little girl."

"She knew she was right," Charlotte said.

"Yes," Mummy said. "But her mummy still didn't believe her. She told the little girl, 'We'll take one more look, just in case.'"

"She found the little girl curled up by the window, gazing out at the dark sea and the moonlight that shone on the shore. 'What are you doing up out of bed?' asked her mummy."

"'There is something down there by the sea. I *know* that there is.' That's what the little girl told her mummy," said Charlotte.

"Yes she did," Mummy said, "and her mummy didn't believe there was. But she thought for a bit and said, 'We'll take a look to make sure.'"

"The little girl had her supper
and her mummy put her to
bed. Later she came to see
if the little girl was asleep."

"But the little girl's bed was
empty," said Charlotte. "The
duvet was thrown right back,
and the little girl wasn't there.
'My goodness, where can she
be?' thought her mummy."

"Something like that," Mummy
said. "Her mummy searched
all over the house."

"I like this bit," Charlotte said.

"It was a little girl," Mummy said. "She had been to a party. The little girl told her mummy she had seen something move in the dark."

"'There's something down there by the boats'," Charlotte said. "That's what the little girl told her mummy."

"Yes," Mummy said. "But her mummy hurried her into the house. She didn't want her to catch cold."

"What happened then?" asked Charlotte.

"Maybe he did. We don't know.
Then a big something came."

"It was a car," Charlotte said.

"I expect the little kitten had never
seen a car before," Mummy said.
"He was scared and he hid. The car
lights shone into the dark. And
there were two shiny bright eyes.
Somebody saw them."

"I know who saw them!"
said Charlotte.

"Once there was a white kitten called Moonlight," Mummy said.

"We don't know he was called Moonlight," Charlotte said. "We just know he got lost."

"That's right," Mummy said, "the little kitten was lost and alone, and wandering about. It was a cold winter night."

"The little kitten was crying," said Charlotte. "Maybe he wanted someone to find him."

"I'd like my story again," Charlotte said.
"Which story?" asked Mummy.
"The one I like best, about Moonlight
   and me," Charlotte said.
"I thought that's the one it might be,"
   Mummy said.

A Kitten
Called
Moonlight

MARTIN WADDELL
illustrated by
CHRISTIAN BIRMINGHAM

WALKER BOOKS
AND SUBSIDIARIES
LONDON · BOSTON · SYDNEY · AUCKLAND

For Charlotte
M W.

For Elizabeth
C.3.

First published 2000 by Walker Books Ltd
87 Vauxhall Walk, London SE11 5HJ

This edition published 2006

10 9 8 7 6 5 4 3

Text © 2000 Martin Waddell
Illustrations © 2000 Christian Birmingham

The right of Martin Waddell and Christian Birmingham to be
identified as author and illustrator respectively of this work has
been asserted by them in accordance with the Copyright, Designs
and Patents Act 1988.

This book has been typeset in Calligraphic.

Printed in China

British Library Cataloguing in Publication Data
A catalogue record for this book is available
from the British Library.

ISBN 978-1-4063-0098-7

www.walker.co.uk

A Kitten
Called
Moonlight

THIS WALKER BOOK BELONGS TO:

_____

_____

_____

WALKER BOOKS is the world's leading independent
publisher of children's books. Working with
the best authors and illustrators we create books
for all ages, from babies to teenagers – books your child
will grow up with and always remember. So…

FOR THE BEST CHILDREN'S BOOKS, LOOK FOR THE BEAR